Series 549

A Ladybird
Robin Hood Adventure

The Ambush

A story by MAX KESTER

Illustrated by
JOHN KENNEY

Publishers : Wills & Hepworth Ltd., Loughborough
First published 1955   ©   *Printed in England*

THE AMBUSH

Early one autumn morning, on a stubble field not far from Sherwood Forest, the peace and quiet was broken by a terrible commotion. The noise was so loud that the woodcutter's wife, in her cottage at the end of the wood, threw down her broom and rushed to the door. What she saw made her quickly go inside again, and bar the door safely! Two soldiers, with the black boar's head which showed they were in the service of Sir Guy of Gisborne, were roughly dragging a poor little man across the stubble field. But it was not the little man, or the soldiers, who were making all the noise. It was a large flock of geese cackling and screaming, flapping their wings and stretching their long necks out as they hissed at the men who were dragging away their owner. Sometimes one fierce old gander would take a nip at the legs of one of the soldiers, only to be kicked aside.

" Pray, masters," quavered the little man, whose name was Goodman Price, " what have I done that you should seize me like this ? "

" What have you done ? " growled one soldier. " Don't you know that the field where your geese have been feeding is the property of our lord and master, Sir Guy of Gisborne ? "

"Aye," snarled the other, " and you are to be taken to the tilting-yard of his castle and whipped soundly."

" But what harm have I done ? " cried Goodman Price. " The field is clear; the corn has been gathered! My geese were only feeding on the stubble to get them fat for Christmas! "

" Ha! " cried the soldier, " you'll never see them again! I *like* goose! " And he licked his lips.

As they passed the cottage, the wood-cutter's wife, with her ear to the door, heard every word they said.

No sooner had the soldiers gone than she darted out of her cottage, locked her door, and picking up her skirts ran through a clearing in the wood till she reached a poor little wattle hut far on the other side. A little, fat old woman was washing her clothes at a spring which bubbled out of the ground, and a few lean pigs were rooting about at the foot of the beech trees. The woodcutter's wife ran up to her and stopped, sadly out of breath.

" Why," exclaimed the fat old woman, with a smile, " how be you, neighbour ? "

The woodcutter's wife wasted no words. " Betsy Price," she cried, " the soldiers— Sir Guy's soldiers—have taken your good man to be whipped—aye, and I heard them say they were coming back for your geese, too! "

Betsy Price gave a great cry. "My man whipped?" she moaned, "and the geese to be taken. But—they're all we have in the world!"

For she knew that Sir Guy was cruel and wicked, and oppressed the poor folk, ruling them with a rod of iron.

"What can we do?" she wailed, throwing her apron over her head, and rocking her fat body to and fro.

But the woodcutter's wife was made of sterner stuff. "No good crying, Betsy," she said, "there's only one man who can help us, as he helps all the poor—Robin Hood!"

Hope shone on fat Betsy's tear-streaked face, then it grew doleful again. "But where can we find him? No man knows his hiding place."

"Come," said the woodcutter's wife. "Come with me!"

Now far across the wood was a big yellow rock, which was the haunt of many jackdaws and ravens. At the foot of the rock was a cave where an old hermit, Simon by name, lived. He was the wisest man for miles around, and the people went to him for medicine and help. But he also had another secret. He was the only man who knew where Robin Hood had his camp —deep in the heart of Sherwood. Many were the tales of distress old Simon had heard and, by passing the word to Robin Hood and his Merry Men, he had saved many poor men from torture or the gallows.

At this very moment old Simon was talking to two men in Lincoln Green, with daggers by their sides and great bows on their backs. One of them was just lowering to the ground a wild boar, which he had been carrying as though it was a feather! This was Little John, the giant of Robin's band, and the other was Robin himself!

"There, Simon," said Robin, "this will feed you for many a day. A fine fat fellow, I warrant!"

Simon was about to thank the two outlaws, when a sound was borne on the gentle breeze which made him stop. It was the sound of a bell!

Without a word—as though they knew the meaning of the sound—the two outlaws slipped inside the cave and Simon, looking round to see that no traces were left, sat down on a little bench outside his cave, and waited.

Some distance away, in a grove of trees, the woodcutter's wife stopped running and grasped Betsy Price by the arm. "Wait!" she said, "we must give the signal." And she went up to a tall tree covered with moss and ivy. Quickly she unwound one of the trails of ivy from its trunk, and gave three sharp pulls. High up in the tree a bell began to ring. Then, after a pause, they walked on in the direction of the cave.

Simon was waiting for them, and their story was soon told. When they had done, he spoke. "You are fortunate," he said gravely, "help is nearer than you think. Now make haste back to your cottage, Mistress Woodcutter, and take Betsy Price with you."

When they had gone, he went into the cave, and as Robin heard the story his handsome face grew dark with anger. "Sir Guy needs a lesson," he said. "Quick, John, we must lose no time."

"I have the disguises here," said old Simon, and going into a dark part of the cave, he brought out two bundles of clothing.

"We must take the short cut, over the meadows," said John, and Robin nodded.

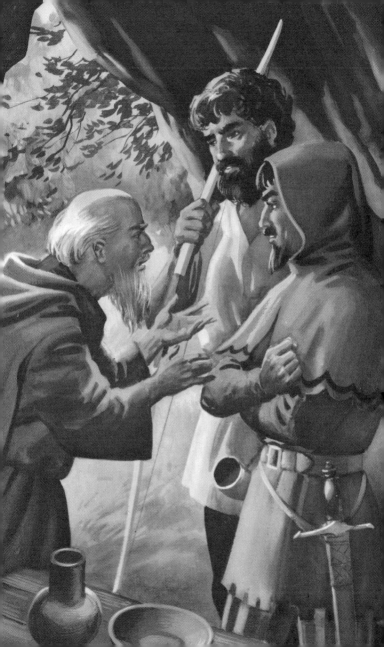

Some time later, on the dusty track which led to the forbidding outer walls of Sir Guy's castle, two shepherds were waiting. They were sitting by the roadside eating bread and cheese with great relish. Suddenly the larger of the shepherds—a giant of a man—stopped with a hunk of bread half-way to his mouth.

" Here they are," he said in a low voice.

" Go on eating," said the other, " wait till they come up to us."

Over the hill came two perspiring soldiers, dragging between them Goodman Price, whose spindly shanks seemed to have given way with fatigue and fright. The two shepherds rose to their feet and advanced to the middle of the roadway.

"Give you good day," said Robin (for of course it was none but he) "have you seen any sheep straying as you came over the hill?"

"We've no time to bother with sheep, or shepherds," answered one of the soldiers. "We're taking this fellow to be whipped soundly."

"Ah," said Little John, putting on a rough voice. "And what dreadful crime has he been up to, eh?"

"He's been feeding his geese on Sir Guy of Gisborne's stubbles."

Robin Hood, turning his head away so that his smile was hidden by his hood, spoke to Goodman Price. "That is a wicked thing to do," he said in a stern voice. "I once saw two men whipped. Two soldiers they were, and"—suddenly both he and Little John lifted their shepherd's crooks—"believe me, master, they never forgot it!"

And with that word the two disguised outlaws brought their crooks smartly down on the backs of the soldiers, and belaboured them so soundly that they never had even time to get their hands to the hilts of their swords.

The first blows were like *this*! And the next like *that!* . . . As down came the crooks—*thwack . . . bang . . . crack !*

How the soldiers howled, trying to protect their heads with their hands! How Goodman Price stood amazed at the turn events had taken!

Soon the soldiers had had enough, and ran helter-skelter towards the castle walls, hotly chased by the two outlaws. As they got near the drawbridge both Robin and John thought discretion was the better part of valour, and the two of them dived into the thick undergrowth and hid, laughing fit to burst their sides.

" What if they turn out the castle guard and search for us ? " said Little John.

" They won't—they'll have to report this business to Sir Guy," chuckled Robin. Then his eyes began to twinkle. " John, will you go back to the cave and bring me my long bow and a couple of good arrows. And wait! " he added as his companion was going bounding off, " tell good old Simon to write this on a piece of parchment . . ." and he whispered something in Little John's ear.

Inside the castle, Sir Guy had seen the two soldiers come in, rubbing their sides and howling, and had sent for them right away.

What they told him made his evil face even more unpleasant.

" What! " he stormed, " you—you let two humble shepherds treat you so! " And he began to beat them himself, with the flat of his sword, until they ran smarting from the room. Then Sir Guy sent for his steward and gave orders that the shepherds should be brought in and hanged from the great gallows in the tilting-yard. But the steward was a man of some experience.

" My lord," he said, when he could get a word between the angry knight's storming and raving. " These were not shepherds, they were members of that meddlesome band of outlaws headed by your enemy Robin Hood! "

"Pooh," shouted the furious Sir Guy. "That miscreant would never dare to venture so near my castle walls."

But—at that very moment—Robin Hood was nearer to the castle walls than Sir Guy had dreamed. Outside the walls grew a tall pine tree, and in the highest branches Robin, the greatest archer in the world, was fitting an arrow to his bow. Down at the foot Little John was calling up to him. "You can never do it!" he cried, "Sir Guy's window is but a slit in the wall, and the distance is too great!"

But Robin laughed, and setting his back against the trunk, took careful aim. Away sped the arrow, but missed the long narrow window by the width of a hand!

" Now you have shot your arrow and wasted the message! " cried Little John. " Not I," said Robin gaily, " that was a sighting shot. Now I know how much the top of the tree sways in the wind, I will allow for it." He drew his great bow to its fullest extent and off sped the second arrow, straight and true, right through the window. Almost before it had entered, Robin was down the tree and both outlaws were scurrying through the undergrowth.

Sir Guy was still berating his steward for thinking the two shepherds were Robin Hood's band, and indeed, was in the middle of a sentence when the arrow fell on the floor at his feet. He turned pale as death, and it was some moments before he could pick it up. With a trembling hand he unrolled the parchment round the shaft. " Beat no more gooseherds or I will beat you, sure as my name is Robin Hood."

With a brow black as thunder the knight rushed to the window, but there was not a soul in sight.

At that moment Sir Guy of Gisborne swore a mighty oath to be revenged on Robin Hood, but he had to wait many weeks before his chance came. It so happened that one day a company of monks stopped at the castle for shelter and food. Sir Guy watched with interest as the pack horses were unloaded. For slung across their saddles were great chests. The Prior of the monastery looked at Sir Guy. " We are founding a new abbey," he said, " and all our gear and goods are in those chests."

" Why," exclaimed Sir Guy, " a man could hide . . ." then he broke off short, for he had suddenly thought of an idea!

The next day, at high noon, Will Scarlett, high up in the branches of the Trysting Oak, deep in the heart of Sherwood Forest, was shading his eyes with his hand when he saw, advancing across the meadows, a cavalcade of horses and men. They looked like monks, clad in black, but there was a frown on cheery Will's face as he dropped to the ground among the ring of outlaws.

" Robin," he said, " here is some booty for us, if I be not mistaken." Robin climbed with him up the tree, and when he saw the black robes he chided Will soundly. " You know we do not rob holy men, Will," he said sharply. " Let them go in peace." But Will clutched him by the arm and bade him look again. " When did you ever see monks marching in step, and striding out as vigorously as trained men-at-arms ? " he said. Robin clapped him on the shoulder, and there was a light in his eye.

" This is a trap," he cried, " but we will be too clever for them yet."

Now among Robin's band was a very fat jolly friar whose name was Friar Tuck. And, indeed, at this very moment he was tucking away into his capacious stomach a large venison pasty. Robin whispered some words to him, and sent him off ahead in the direction the procession of monks was taking.

Now this particular way would have to pass through a thick grove of overhanging trees which shaded a green walk by the side of a deep river, and Robin knew this. He gathered his band round him, and gave them quick instructions. Soon there was not a man in sight.

Away in the distance the procession was approaching the grove of trees, but while they were still a long way off, the fat figure of Friar Tuck emerged from the trees.

He was leaning heavily on his staff, and pretending to be tired. "Alms, for the love of sweet Charity!" he called out in a whining voice. As he stood right in the middle of their way the procession had to halt.

"Out of our way, fellow!" cried the leader of the cavalcade of monks in a rough and far from saintly voice.

"Give me but a penny, sirs," whined the friar, "I am sure you have plenty and to spare in your chests here."

The leader thrust him angrily aside and signalled for the troop to move on under the trees. They were all beneath the overhanging branches when—zin—n-n gg!—there was the twang of a bowstring, and the leader (who was no other than Sir Guy's steward) was struck in the chest by an arrow aimed by an invisible hand.

But it did not pierce him to the heart; it clattered to the ground because of the coat of mail the supposed monk wore under his robes.

"Aha," cried a ringing voice from the depth of the woods. "A trap, eh? As I thought!"

And the shrill notes of a silver horn rang through the forest.

Almost as if by magic a score of lithe green clad figures fell from the branches of the overhanging trees in which they had been concealed. The monks were thrown into confusion. They tried to fumble under their robes to get at their daggers, but they seemed surrounded by a mass of leaping men and soon they were trussed up with ropes. Then into the glade strode a tall figure, bow in hand. Quickly Robin Hood went up to the steward and tore his monkish robe off his shoulders, disclosing a wad of mail.

"A monk, are you? Since when has Sir Guy's steward become a holy man?" he scoffed.

Now, as we know, Sir Guy and his steward had discussed very carefully the plan to trap Robin Hood, and both of them had expected this attack, and the wily steward knew what to say.

"Good Robin Hood," he said, "we will do you no harm. We dressed up as monks in order to carry our treasure safely through the forest, for we knew you would not attack holy men. But since you have discovered our trick, take the treasure and let us go."

Robin Hood stood for a moment. He didn't know what to make of this. A man like Sir Guy would not give up treasure without a fight. He called Little John to his side. "What shall we do?" he asked. John had his answer ready. "Why, good Robin, let us take the treasure, we can use it to help the poor."

" If it *is* treasure," replied Robin thought-fully. " Here, open this first chest." No sooner said than done, and the big box was taken down and opened. It was full of small leather bags, and from the topmost bag came the chink of money.

" It *is* treasure all right!" cried the delighted Little John.

But Robin was not satisfied. " Take them all off the horses, and then send these rascals back to their master," he ordered.

The chests were placed in a row by the river bank, and then Little John ordered the outlaws to each notch an arrow to their bows.

Then the men-at-arms were released from their bonds. " Harken, fellows," cried Robin, " when I have counted ten, my merry men shall let loose their arrows! So," he added with a grin, " the fastest runner will be safest! "

Hardly had he started counting before the men-at-arms were scampering off as fast as their legs would carry them while the outlaws, splitting their sides with laughter, shot arrows at their legs and jeered at them till they were out of sight.

" No more! " cried Robin at last. " Let us carry these treasure chests back to the Trysting Oak, where we may empty them safely! "

As they went to the river's edge to begin picking up the chests one of the outlaws noticed a very queer thing. The chest he was looking at had a lot of holes bored in it. He called Robin over. Robin took a careful look, and then went to the other chests. They were all the same, except the chest with the bags of gold in it, which had *no* holes in it. Robin put his ear to the holes in one of the chests and to his surprise he distinctly heard the sound of heavy breathing!

He raised the lid the merest trifle—it was not locked! He stood up. "These chests are heavy," he said loudly, "let the horses carry them back to our hiding place for us."

Then he went round whispering to the outlaws, and each one started to chuckle. However, they quietly slung the chests on the horses sides, and then, with broad smiles on their faces, drove the laden animals into the deepest part of the river! Soon the water began to flow into the holes, and it was not long before a cry came from one of the chests.

"Help, I am drowning! Help!

"By my faith," cried Robin, pretending to be frightened, "these chests are bewitched. The gold and treasure is enchanted! We will have none of it. Cut it loose, at once!"

One by one the chests were slashed loose, and fell into the river. Up popped the lids, and out came—not treasure—but soldiers!

As quick as lightning the outlaws ranged themselves on the bank of the river, and threw turves and clods at the miserable splashing men. Try as they might, the soldiers could not climb up on to the bank, but were forced to wade and swim downstream while the laughing outlaws ran alongside.

It was a wet and bedraggled band of soldiers who arrived that night at Sir Guy of Gisborne's castle. What their lord and master said to them no man knows, but the lightning and thunder that broke over the castle was no ordinary storm. People said it was Sir Guy exploding!

Series 549